# Little Puff

A Beginning-to-Read Book

# Little Puff

## by Margaret Hillert
### Illustrated by Sid Jordan

**DEAR CAREGIVER,** The *Beginning-to-Read* series is a carefully written collection of classic readers you may remember from your own childhood. Each book features text comprised of common sight words to provide your child ample practice reading the words that appear most frequently in written text. The many additional details in the pictures enhance the story and offer the opportunity for you to help your child expand oral language and develop comprehension.

Begin by reading the story to your child, followed by letting him or her read familiar words and soon your child will be able to read the story independently. At each step of the way, be sure to praise your reader's efforts to build his or her confidence as an independent reader. Discuss the pictures and encourage your child to make connections between the story and his or her own life. At the end of the story, you will find reading activities and a word list that will help your child practice and strengthen beginning reading skills.

Above all, the most important part of the reading experience is to have fun and enjoy it!

*Shannon Cannon*

Shannon Cannon,
Literacy Consultant

Norwood House Press • P.O. Box 316598 • Chicago, Illinois 60631
For more information about Norwood House Press please visit our website at
*www.norwoodhousepress.com* or call 866-565-2900.

**LIBRARY OF CONGRESS CATALOGING-IN-PUBLICATION DATA**
Hillert, Margaret.
 Little Puff / Margaret Hillert ; illustrated by Sid Jordan. — Rev. and expanded library ed.
 p. cm. — (Beginning-to-read series)
 Summary: "After jumping the track to search for companionship, a little train finally finds a place in the zoo"--Provided by publisher.
 ISBN-13: 978-1-59953-185-4 (library edition : alk. paper)
 ISBN-10: 1-59953-185-2 (library edition : alk. paper)  1. Readers (Primary) [1. Railroads—Trains—Fiction.] I. Jordan, Sid, ill. II. Title.
 PE1119.H579 2008
 [E]—dc22                              2008001642

See me.
Big, big me.
Look at big red me.

See my little cars.
One, two, three.
One blue car.
One yellow car.
And one that is red.

6

But no one is here with me.
I do not like it here.
I guess I will look for something.

Here I go.
Jump, jump, jump to see
what I can see.

I can puff, puff, puff.
I can go away.
Away, away, away.

Puff—puff—.
Here I go.
Up—and up—and up!

Puff, puff.
Here I come.
Down,
    down,
        down,
            down,
                down!

Here comes something.
Look at this.
Look at this.
What is it?

We do not want you.
You can not come in here.
Go away.

Oh, no!
Look at this!
You can not do this!

14

Get away.
Get away.
This will not work.
We do not want you here.

Where can I go?
No one wants me.
Where can I go now?

What is this?
It looks like fun.
I guess I will go in here.

17

Oh, my.
What do I see here?
It is something big, big, big.

And look up here.
Look up, up, up.
Here is a big one, too.
A big one with spots.

Oh, oh.
Look in here.
Here is something funny.
The funny little ones can play.

Look at the mother.
A little one is with the mother.
I like this little one.

Oh, Little Puff.
Come here. Come here.
Help, help.
We want you.
You can help us.

You can work for us.
You can play with us.
We can ride with you.
What fun! What fun!

Ride with me.
Come ride with me.
Get in, get in, get in.

Now, this is fun.
I like it here.
I like this work.
This is the spot for me.

25

# READING REINFORCEMENT

The following activities support the findings of the National Reading Panel that determined the most effective components for reading instruction are: Phonemic Awareness, Phonics, Vocabulary, Fluency, and Text Comprehension.

## Phonemic Awareness: Syllabication

Say the following words, clapping the syllables as you say them. Ask your child to tell you how many syllables are in each word:

| | | |
|---|---|---|
| little-2 | away-2 | yellow-2 |
| big-1 | like-1 | puff-1 |
| up-1 | guess-1 | something-2 |
| giraffe-2 | tracks-1 | rooster-2 |
| elephant-3 | monkeys-2 | tiger-2 |
| children-2 | zoo-1 | mother-2 |

## Phonics: Syllabication

1. Write the following word parts on separate index cards. Display the syllables for each word, out of order, and help your child put them together to make words:

| | | | | |
|---|---|---|---|---|
| lit/tle | a/way | yel/low | moth/er | sta/tion |
| child/ren | mon/keys | some/thing | el/e/phant | po/lice |

## Vocabulary: Personal Pronouns

1. Explain to your child that words that can be substituted for the names of people are called pronouns.

2. Write the following pronouns on separate pieces of paper:

    me      I      we      you      us

3. Read each pronoun to your child and ask your child to repeat it.

4. Mix the words up. Point to a word and ask your child to read it. Provide clues if your child needs them.

5. Read the following sentences to your child. Ask your child to provide an appropriate pronoun to complete the sentence.

   • Little Puff said, "Look at big red _____." (me)

   • Little Puff was lonely and said, "_____ guess_____ will go look for something." (I/I)

   • The animals said, "_____ do not want _____ here." (We/you)

   • The children at the zoo said, "_____ can help _____." (You/us)

   • Little Puff said, "This is the spot for _____." (me)

## Fluency: Choral Reading

1. Reread the story with your child at least two more times while your child tracks the print by running a finger under the words as they are read. Ask your child to read the words he or she knows with you.

2. Reread the story aloud together. Be careful to read at a rate that your child can keep up with.

3. Repeat choral reading and allow your child to be the lead reader. Ask him or her to change from a whisper to a loud voice while you follow along and change your voice.

## Text Comprehension: Discussion Time

1. Ask your child to retell the sequence of events in the story.

2. To check comprehension, ask your child the following questions:

   • Why did Little Puff leave the train tracks?

   • How do you think Little Puff felt when the people in the town said they didn't want or need Little Puff?

   • What kinds of animals did Little Puff see? Which animals live on a farm? Which animals live in the zoo?

   • Do you think Little Puff is happy at the zoo? Why or why not?

**Little Puff uses the 61 words listed below.**
This list can be used to practice reading the words that appear in the text. You may wish to write the words on index cards and use them to help your child build automatic word recognition. Regular practice with these words will enhance your child's fluency in reading connected text.

| | | | |
|---|---|---|---|
| a | get | my | the |
| and | go | | this |
| at | guess | no | three |
| away | | not | to |
| | help | now | too |
| big | here | | two |
| blue | | oh | |
| but | I | one(s) | up |
| | in | | us |
| can | is | play | |
| car(s) | it | puff | want(s) |
| come(s) | | | we |
| | jump | red | what |
| do | | ride | where |
| down | like | | will |
| | little | see | with |
| for | look(s) | something | work |
| fun | | spot(s) | |
| funny | me | | yellow |
| | mother | that | you |

**ABOUT THE AUTHOR** Margaret Hillert has written over 80 books for children who are just learning to read. Her books have been translated into many different languages and over a million children throughout the world have read her books. She first started writing poetry as a child and has continued to write for children and adults throughout her life. A first grade teacher for 34 years, Margaret is now retired from teaching and lives in Michigan where she likes to write, take walks in the morning, and care for her three cats.

Photograph by Glenna Washburn

**ABOUT THE ADVISER** Shannon Cannon contributed the activities pages that appear in this book. Shannon serves as a literacy consultant and provides staff development to help improve reading instruction. She is a frequent presenter at educational conferences and workshops. Prior to this she worked as an elementary school teacher and as president of a curriculum publishing company.